Eating Food

Written by Jo Windsor

Rigby

In this book you will see animals eating food.

You will see...

claws

jaws

straws

Some bugs like to eat meat.

This bug has two big claws!
It comes out at night to get its food.

It gets its food with its big claws.

Those are very big claws!

claw

This insect likes to eat meat, too.
It has an insect to eat.

It eats the insect with its big jaws.

This bug eats...

bugs Yes? No?

birds Yes? No?

grass Yes? No?

jaws

This jellyfish likes to eat meat.

It is eating a fish.

The jellyfish pulls the fish into its mouth.

fish inside
the jellyfish

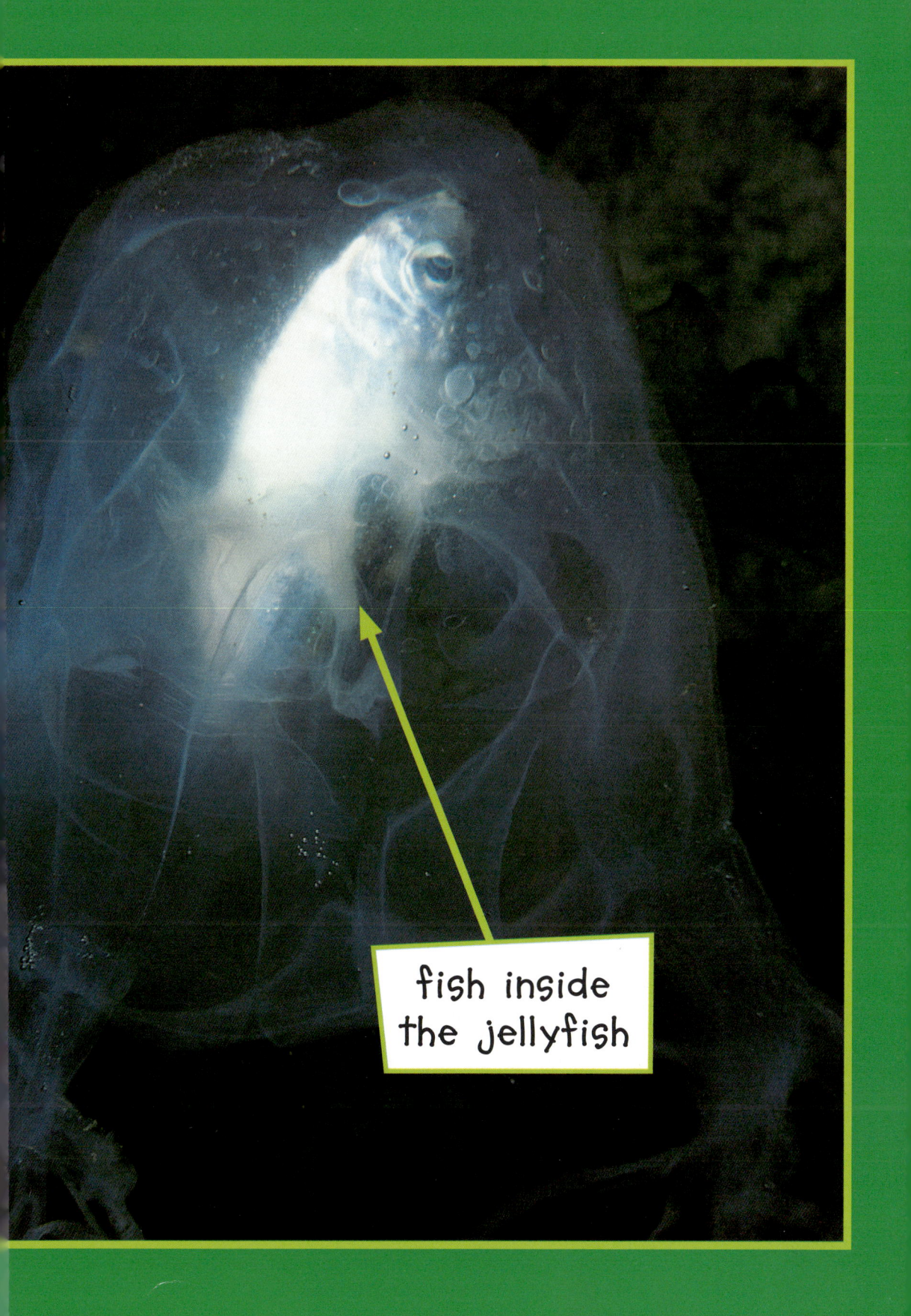

This crab has one claw
that is bigger than the rest.
The big claw is for getting the food.

Look, a fish!

The crab has the fish in its big claw.

This crab gets
its food with...

a big claw   Yes? No?

a little claw   Yes? No?

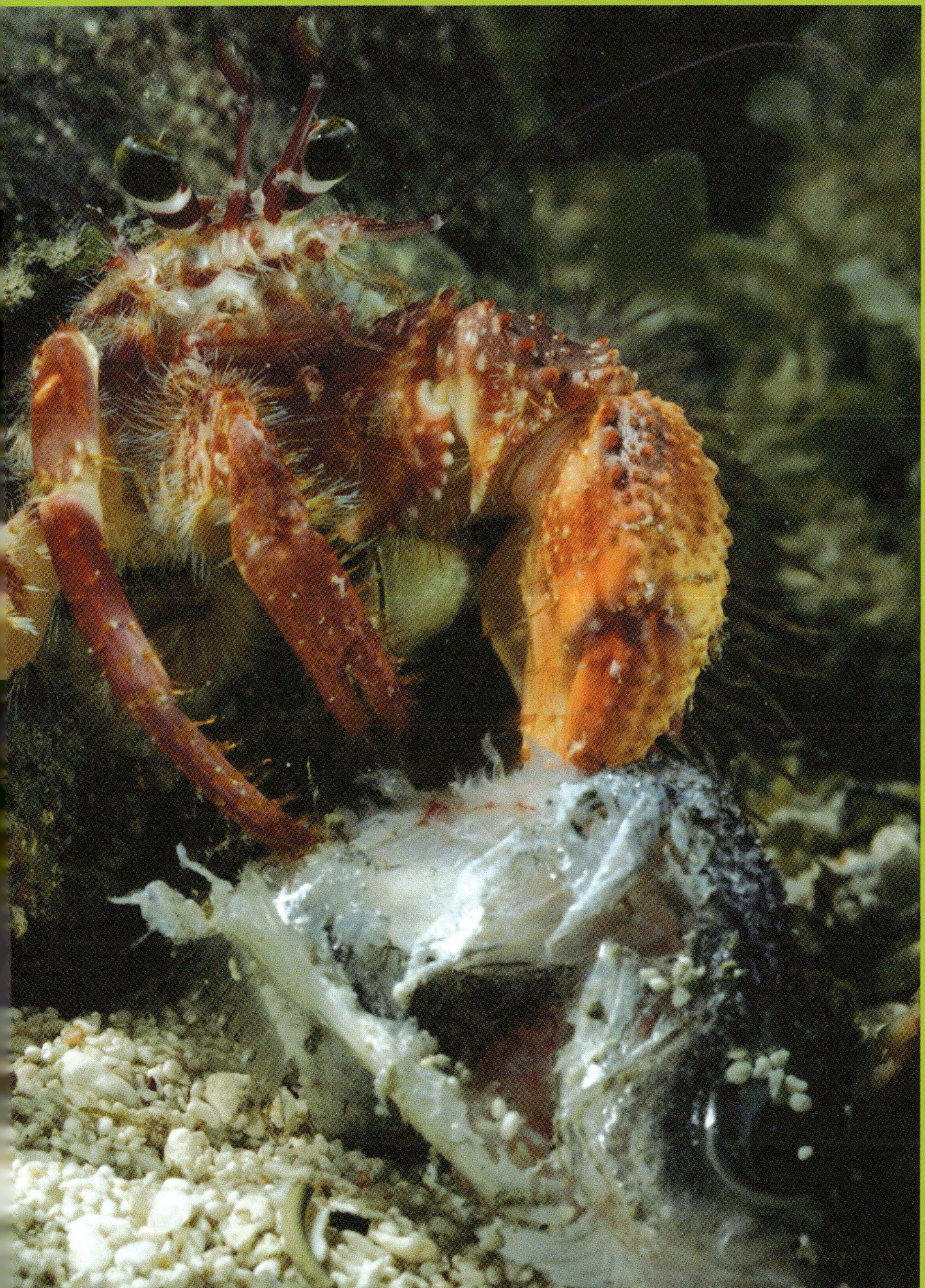

Some bugs like to eat plants.

This bug is eating a plant. It can eat the leaves.

This bug looks like the plant! Other insects won't see it when it is getting its food.

Other insects will…

eat the plant — Yes? No?

eat the insect — Yes? No?

13

These are shellfish.

They are on the rocks.

They do not hunt for food.

They stay on the rocks and get little bits of food that are in the water.

The shellfish gets food from...

the air   Yes? No?

the water   Yes? No?

the rocks   Yes? No?

15

Some insects like to drink their food.

This butterfly is on a flower.
It has a mouth like a straw.
It will get the food from the flower.

The butterfly gets its food from...

the air   Yes? No?

the flower Yes? No?

butterfly's mouth

17

This bird likes to drink from a flower, too.

It puts its beak into the flower.

It gets the food out with its tongue.

Animals get food...

with a claw   Yes? No?

with a tail   Yes? No?

with a tongue   Yes? No?

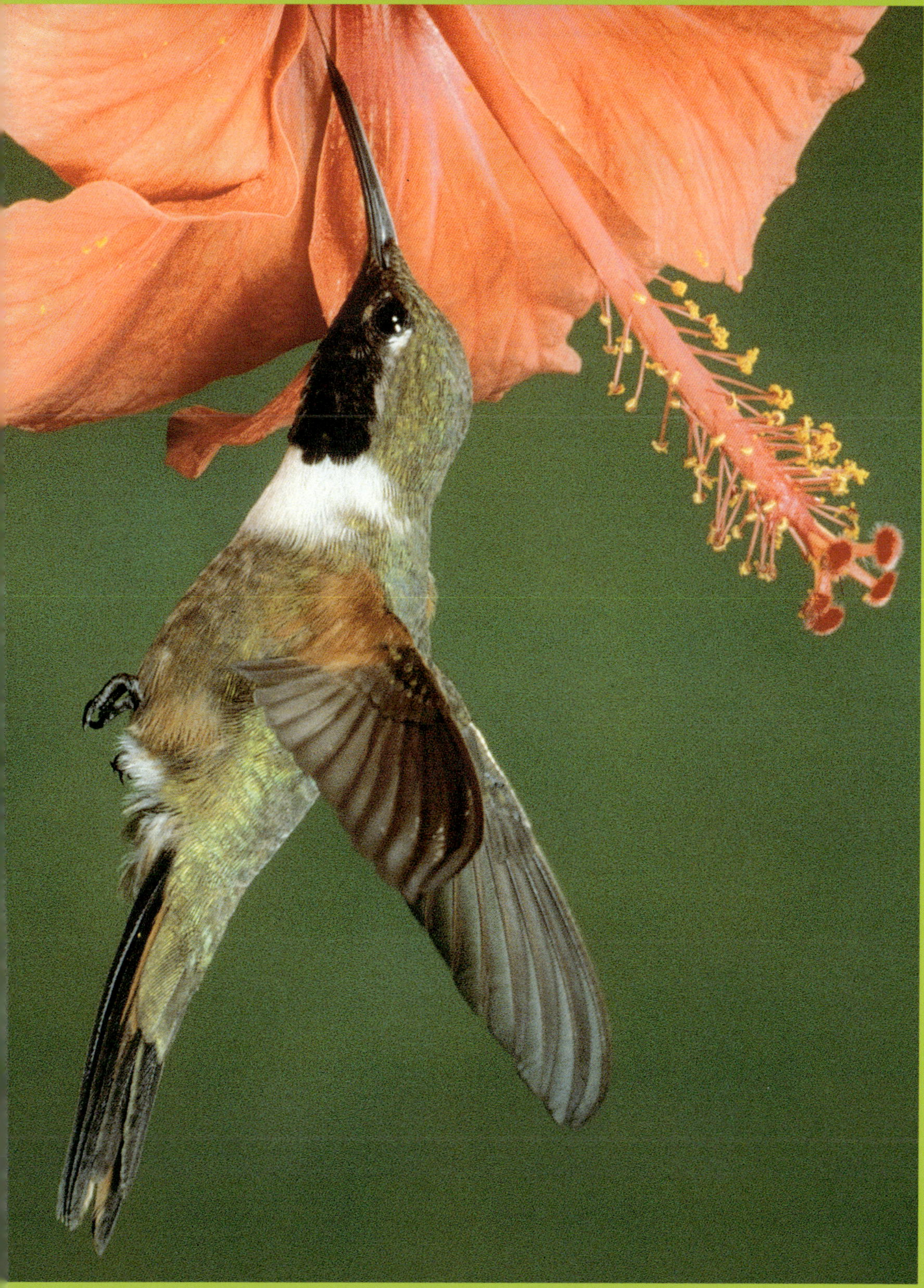

This fly is getting food, too.

It is getting food with its tongue!

Look out!

Flies can eat your dinner!

tongue

Index

birds 18

bugs . . . 4, 6, 12, 20

butterflies 16

claws 3, 4, 10

crabs 10

jaws 3, 6

jellyfish 8

shellfish 14

tongues 18, 20

Mapping chart

Match the pictures.

insect

bird

crab

claw	flower
jaw	fish
beak	insect

Word Bank

beak

fish

flower

insect

leaves

plant

rock

straw

tongue